UNDER THE SEAL

UNDER THE SEAL

by

Carol Mauriello

Accents Publishing • Lexington, Kentucky • 2021

Printed in the United States of America

Accents Publishing
Editor: Katerina Stoykova-Klemer
Cover Image: Photo by Maksim ŠiŠlo on *Unsplash*

Library of Congress Control Number: 2021948258
ISBN: 978-1-936628-85-8
First Edition

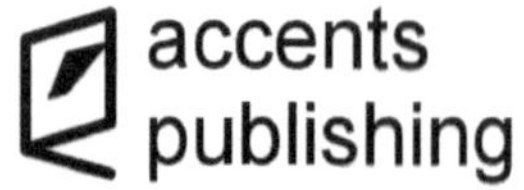

Accents Publishing is an independent press for brilliant voices. For a catalog of current and upcoming titles, please visit us on the Web at

www.accents-publishing.com

For Joe

1

Wendell

Patsy Ann Singleton, Wendell Troy thought, was a damned good-looking woman. What was she? Forty? Maybe older. He had been out with older women before. Hell, he'd been out with hundreds of women, many of them older.

"What do you say I take you home, Doc?" he offered. He was fiddling with a little Buddha she kept on her desk.

She looked at him with that knowing smile and her head tilted in a way that tossed her short brown curls just slightly, all of it evoking something in him he couldn't quite describe, except that it made him want her. She had changed somehow from the first time he'd seen her a year ago, but he couldn't put his finger on what that was exactly either. She had begun to dress differently lately, but that wasn't all of it. Maybe it was an attitude that made her sexier. He was familiar with attitude. He tried to see what she was seeing in front of her—a nineteen-year-old, good-looking young guy—He filled out his t-shirt and jeans like a James Dean. Many women had told him that. He'd rented some old movies to check him out. He smiled at her, letting the cigarette he'd just lit dangle from his mouth. She was old enough to know who James Dean was. He imagined her at 14 with all those magazine covers on the wall of her bedroom.

She smiled back. "No, Wendell. I've got reports that'll keep me here late," she said. "Please put out the cigarette. And don't call me Doc."

She had to be like that, he thought. At least to pretend to enforce the rules. After all, she was a professional, but if he could be alone with her long enough, he could break down that professional bullshit. He looked at her, squinting one eye through the smoke, but she had her head down checking her notes. "Are you a Buddhist?" he asked, nodding at the little statue he now held in his hand.

"No," she said. I'm Catholic." She sighed with a long, deep breath. "At least I was born one."

He looked at her, waiting for more. "A lapsed one? Catholic, I mean."

She looked at him as if trying to figure out how much to tell him. Then she took a deep breath before answering. "That's a little token I picked up somewhere, the Buddha that is. I just liked it, so I bought it. I don't really know why."

"Who knows why we do anything we do? Right, Doc? Like that painting there?" he said, indicating an abstract on the wall that looked expensive. "That's new. Wasn't here last month."

"Sure, like the painting. I'm not any expert on modern art or anything, and people would say it's not really *me*, but—" She glanced over her shoulder at it. "I'll have to admit, it's different."

Wendell nodded and rose to go, but then hesitated at the door. "I can wait for you," he said, suddenly turning and sitting down on one of the stiff vinyl chairs near the door. He picked up a magazine. "I won't talk; I'll just wait." He was breaking her down, he knew. Just a little more nudging, gentle-like, not forcing himself. She was ready; he could tell. It was just a matter of some coaxing.

"No," she said. "Absolutely not." She had a pencil in her hand and pointed it at him. "I'll put you down for four o'clock next week? Is that all right?"

"Always the professional," he said, "aren't you?"

She glanced back at him. "Yes."

"Well, I can see through that," he said, picking up a magazine and flipping through it quickly. He was running out of time. If he wanted her, he was going to have to push harder. "Your husband shouldn't leave you here alone at night. It's dangerous. I'd never let any wife of mine—"

"The doors are locked, Wendell. I'm perfectly safe."

He looked at her for a moment, not saying anything. Finally, he said, "I'm not coming back, Ms. Singleton." That would surely get her attention.

"But you have to. The court has ordered you to complete your therapy—otherwise you go back to jail."

"If they catch me," he said.

The phone rang and they both looked at it. Wendell Troy stood, turned his back to her, and opened the door again. "Gotta go," he said.

"Wait, Wendell. Wait just a moment. We have to talk."

I've got her in my pocket now, he said to himself.

"Hello," she breathed into the phone. Maybe she wasn't aware of how sexy her voice was, or maybe she was expecting a call.

"Oh, it's you," she said. There was a softening in her voice. When he turned around, Wendell thought he could see a visible change in her face as well—this was probably not her husband, but it was someone important to her. She had no children he knew of, but then she didn't talk about her husband either. She whispered so that he could barely hear, but there was something desperate in her tone when she said, "I—I can't.... No, no, no, you mustn't.... Well, listen, can I call you back? ... Please?"

Wendell coughed to remind her of his presence when she hung up. Whoever it was had really thrown her for a loop. Her face was flushed, and she seemed still engaged with the conversation just ended.

Miz Singleton," he said. She looked up at him.

"I've really got to leave town," he finally said. For a moment she seemed to have forgotten his existence completely, or even what they had been discussing. He watched her come out of the fog and slowly rise to the realization she had a client in front of her. When he thought he had her attention, he said," My family—well you know we're sort of in the cash crop business—I guess you probably know that—we'll be setting up shop somewhere else. That's why I'm not coming back. It's time to leave," he said.

"Wendell, you can get out of that business altogether. You're smart enough and ambitious enough—" She had returned to him. The phone call was in the background now. "You're a very bright young man. We've gone over all this before. Why do you want to throw it all away and wind up in jail?"

"It's not your concern anymore." When she didn't answer, just looked at him in that sad way she had sometimes, he thought he'd try again. "Are you sure I can't take you home? I won't try anything. I promise. I'll be a perfect gentleman."

"It's OK. My husband is picking me up when I'm done."

Wendell sighed, turned, and walked out. "See you in my dreams, Doc."

But he did wait. He waited outside the door and listened, though he couldn't say why. There were not many women who were immune to his charms. Some took a little longer is all, and he'd have to have a little more patience. The door slightly ajar, he heard her dial a number. "Oh, no, it was absolutely … wonderful … Well, you can't just do that … No, no, we have to talk … I have to see you!" And then Wendell couldn't hear anything else except "Meet me there, *please*." And then she hung up. He waited a few more minutes. Suddenly the computer keys started up again as he left the building.

2

Les

Lester Reese fumbled for the phone and then looked at the clock. Two in the morning. "Yeah?" he answered groggily into the receiver. Rosemarie rolled over and groaned a sort of sensuous murmur. He caressed her rounded rump beneath the covers, and ran his free hand over the pale yellow, nearly sheer nightgown she wore. Once again, he wanted the woman lying next to him. He had been convinced that marriage would ruin a man's life, especially a policeman's. Reese couldn't remember when he hadn't been a cop first and last—the women had come and gone in Chicago. But now, seven years and two sons later, he still lusted for his Spanish Rose, as he called her. The boys had inherited her dark good looks, but they were tall, like him. He had what he had always imagined being a "rugged" look about him; his fair skin was nearly always flushed, sanguine beneath his salt-and-pepper hair. And he was proud of the fact he kept himself in pretty good shape at forty-nine, as good as any rookie, or nearly so.

"Detective?" the familiar voice at the other end said.

"What's up, Jake?" Reese responded, sinking back on the pillow as Rosemarie sleepily nuzzled into the curve of his arm. Sometimes he was glad for the decision he had made to return to the rather closed community of Mazewood, Kentucky, to take on a job in the small river town of his birth; he certainly was less tense, more relaxed than he had been in years, but there was a price to pay, as there always was.

"Sh-o-o-o-ting, sir," the dispatch drawled out the double "o" in an almost leisurely fashion. Reese's mind went to the west end of town, a domestic dispute no doubt, he surmised. His mind conjured up the messy house, the beer drinking husband in a torn t-shirt and jeans shooting up the place....

"Anybody hurt?" Reese asked routinely.

"Lady's in pretty bad shape at Pathright Psychiatric Center."

Reese listened to the rest of the report, his jaw tightening.

"What's wrong, Les?" Rosemarie whispered, suddenly fully awake and sitting up, her brown eyes wide, searching his. Her habit of staying awake all night and waiting for him to return when he had night duty was beginning to subside in the nine months since they had moved to Mazewood. Other things about Mazewood disturbed her but she adapted well to the low-stress lifestyle; her pressures were more in the subtleties of culture differences.

Les held up his hand, palm vertical, their code for *it's a problem but nothing to do with us.* Rosemarie's face softened and she nestled her head on his chest again while he spoke briefly to headquarters.

"Got to go, huh?" she asked sadly when he had hung up.

"Don't want to," he said, holding her close to him. "Don't want to at all, but this is my detail." He released her and smiled quickly.

She nodded, understanding.

"What do you suppose the odds are that I would lust after my wife after seven years?" he said playfully swatting her behind as he rose from the bed.

"I wish you could stay home today," she said petulantly. "The boys wanted—"

"Me too." Reese interrupted, leaving her for the bathroom. "But police business comes first; you know that Hon," he said over his shoulder. "Even in Mazewood people get murdered, and I don't mean metaphorically," he added before he disappeared inside and splashed cold water on his face.

"I'll get you some coffee, sweetheart," Rosemarie Marquez Reese offered in her softly accented Spanish, in a voice that always sounded to Reese like a very young girl's. She would never be able to rid herself of that "loving a man means serving him" attitude and he wondered if he really wanted her to.

She began hurrying to the balustrade of the old house they were in the process of redoing. He was proud of the fact he had taken on the sometimes-daunting project; it was something to do in a small town that didn't have much in the line of cultural advantages or sports to hold his attention. The boys helped and it was fun.

"Don't bother with the coffee, Rosie," he said, poking his head out of the bedroom door.

She stopped at the stairwell and looked at him questioningly. One of her paintings framed her hair; colorful circular brushstrokes swooping out like a brilliant halo surrounded her head. Rosie was an artist, the kind a lot of people in town misunderstood. She had been all excited about being part of a juried art show in Mazewood but only one person had liked her work. Lester tried to comfort her, explain the reaction of small-town people to her rather wild and sensual brand of abstract art, but she was hurt.

"I'll pick up some gourmet at the Speedway," he joked. "There's an all-nighter right by the counseling center."

Rosemarie, ignoring the gourmet remark, had already been descending the stairs to put on the brew when she turned, surprised. "Counseling center? Pathright Center? That's where the murder took place? Pathright?" She rejoined him in the bedroom.

"Yeah." His pants on but still unzipped, Reese grabbed

a shirt with buttoned-down collar and slid his feet into the waiting shoes at the side of the bed. Seconds later he rattled the hangers in the closet. "Rosie, have you seen my gray sports jacket—oh, there it is." He whipped it out of the closet and quickly put it on. He kissed her, quick and hard, and then said, "Gotta run; we'll talk later." He was down the hall and opening the door to the boys' room to have a reassuring look, as was his habit, regardless of his hurry. Rosemarie followed him and stopped him downstairs, holding his arm.

"*Who?* Les?" she insisted, and then held her breath. When he didn't immediately respond, she asked again. "Who was killed?"

"They found a woman, an employee. I don't think you know her though. Patsy Singleton. Wife of that uh … coin dealer on Second Street—Bill Singleton. You know I went to high school with him. And she's not dead … not yet anyway." His wife took a deep breath and let a long sigh escape.

"Be careful, Les," she said, a frown beginning to wrinkle her pretty forehead.

3

Cottrell

John Cottrell hung up the phone from the coroner and immediately, as if it were simply a reflex by now, opened the bottom drawer of his highly polished cherry desk and took out a bottle of Absolut and a highball glass, part of the "emergency kit" he kept handy for consolation—his own, naturally—but also for others in their time of grief, when and if he deemed it necessary or appropriate. He prided himself on knowing who was a teetotaler and who was a lush; in fact, he prided himself on not only knowing but keeping his mouth shut—decorum he called it. He was good at his job. Rose to the occasion, no matter how many vodkas he'd had or hadn't had in a day's time. How many people could say that?

The body would be delivered to Cottrell Funeral Home at eleven or so today. He shivered and put on what he thought of as his shield, an undertaker's immunity to the shock of anyone's demise. He had been in the death business for some thirty-odd years, not including the cadavers he'd had to deal with in medical school, but he still was not used to the corpses that had not died by natural causes—those maimed bodies from car accidents and other victims, like Patsy Singleton, who were the targets of senseless killings. It happened though—the violence, sometimes a sick and sordid kind—even in sleepy river towns like Mazewood, Kentucky. Cottrell was glad he did not live in a city where most of the people he worked on he would not have known in life—there was something comforting about *knowing* them. He'd remember them as he worked on them, even talk to them sometimes. After all, there was not much difference in a body alive or recently dead—it had just stopped breathing. He liked to think of the soul sticking around for a time, at least to enjoy the funerals he worked so hard to make just right. He'd have to bring that one up with Gene later.

Luckily, he always worked alone, especially now that his wife was gone. He got to talking more and more to the corpses and wondered if it was a lonely bachelor occupation or just an aging kind of thing where you were mostly in the past when the rest of the world, the baby boomers or whatever they were—the ones with the computers, the cell phones, and the two-income households—were passing you by.

Cottrell sighed and thought about the victim again. He would steel himself with another Absolut before she arrived. The coroner had said that little Patsy (he couldn't help but call her that, though she was in her forties), had died of a clean bullet wound from a .22 right into the chest cavity, at close range, the force splintering a rib and literally tearing her internal organs to pieces. Only one shot, but a .22 bullet will spread out lead inside a person to beat anything you ever saw. Cottrell knew that as well as anyone. He was familiar with coroner's reports and had run for coroner last election at the suggestion of the mayor but was secretly glad he'd been beaten. Bill would want an open casket, he imagined. Her face would be fine for that, but Bill would want her to be holding a rosary, so he'd have to do some work on the chest cavity. She'd have to look natural, like she was sleeping.

It was amazing to think Patsy had hung on as long as she did; she died right on the operating table in Mazewood Hospital's new wing. "For crying out loud," Cottrell had exclaimed in disbelief when he had first heard about it, "they just finished building that damn wing a week or two ago, and now Patsy's gone and christened it—died in it, for Chrissakes. His hand shook as he poured himself another shot. When had his hands started shaking so badly? He really should cut back during the day, maybe just a drink or two with Gene in the evenings. He'd have to get serious about the drinking. Gene Wallace had performed the last rights and wound up at his place afterwards, more upset than he'd ever seen him— maybe he was just showing his age like the rest of us, he thought. The rectory had reached the assistant pastor by cell phone while he sat in Cottrell's kitchen, lamenting over the two vices he still did not have a handle on—he smoked two packs of Camels a day and God knows the amount of alcohol he consumed. Wine at mass didn't count—he hated that stuff!

The Singletons belonged to St. Ann's Catholic Church. Father Gene Wallace, though his title was assistant pastor, did all the leg work in the parish except taking care of the checkbook—that was the pastor's charge. Gene had been called to administer the last sacraments before Patsy Ann Singleton expired. After waking Cottrell at three a.m., when it was over, the priest had needed to talk, to confess, as it were—right there at Cottrell's desk where clergy and undertaker consumed the bottle that now lay at the bottom of the garbage pail outside, covered by kitchen scraps and junk mail. It amused Cottrell to think he, raised to be Protestant, was closer to a Catholic priest than just about anyone else in the world, including members of his own family.

Family? he mused. What was family anyway? They were all gone—his boys, John, Jr. was in medical school and costing him a fortune in tuition, but he'd make it all the way, unlike his father; and Peter, the quiet one, had become an accountant and married a girl from Chicago. (One of them at least might have taken over his lucrative business, but now it seemed out of the question. It would probably die with him.) Truth be told, even Catherine had never liked being a funeral director's wife, though she put up with it for a long time. People often had odd requests for an undertaker—they'd want him to put things into the casket with their loved ones, and that was all right, he'd tell them; he'd buried letters unopened, money, cigars, you name it. When Catherine found out that he was taking it upon himself to send people on to their reward with his own ideas of what they should have, she hit the roof. Still, he didn't see what was wrong with it. The one she really got upset about was Tom Wooley. Poor old man was all alone, and he'd always liked the seamier magazines, so when Wooley died, Cottrell bought up a slew of *Playboy* from the Mazewood Library when they were getting rid of their old publications of the magazine they kept under the desk. Pallbearers never could figure out what made that coffin so heavy. Cottrell laughed at the memory of it. Catherine never did have a sense of humor about the business, much less any understanding of what people really cared about. It was not all about decorum but the appearance of it. He poured still another glass and quaffed it.

Looking down at his shirt front to straighten an errant tie, Cottrell inadvertently caught sight of his own protruding gut brushing against the desk front. Another habit that had gotten out of control, indulging in fatty foods and eating out. Well, Catherine had stopped cooking, even before she left, and he had taken to ordering in pizza when he worked on the bodies. Then and there he decided that, once this bottle of vodka was empty, it would be his last indulgence for a while. The undertaker loosened his belt, put it in the next notch and re-buckled it. When and how had he gotten so terribly fat? he wondered. "Salad for lunch," he said to himself. "Every day next week," he said with finality. He would try to give up booze, but he knew better than to say it out loud. He would not last out the week on that one. Booze got him over the rough spots of his loneliness. Hell, it was just his way of dealing with life. Everybody had to find his own way, didn't he? Picking up the phone, he dialed Bill Singleton's home number.

"I know this is hard for you," he heard himself say, "but we must take care of a few details, son. The body—Patsy's body—will be here soon. There's the business of her clothing ... "He waited for a response but hearing none said, "And a recent picture ... for Margaret Sue to go by ... you know. You know how she is—she's getting old and can't see so well."

Cottrell waited in more of the uncomfortable silence before the man spoke. "Uhm-m, clothing?"

Bill sounded dazed. It was natural, of course, that he would be under stress. Cottrell silently forgave him. Such a shock to the poor man. A terrible, criminal thing to have happened. The police had no doubt already questioned Bill about it, where he was at the time and all, and then he would probably have been at the hospital most of the night. "Such an awful thing," he heard himself say aloud. "So meaningless. I'm so sorry, Bill."

Some lunatic, he surmised, an intruder breaking

into her office where she was working late at night for God knows what—drug money or something. Probably one of the long-haired crazies that you see around town so much these days with earrings in their noses, and other places, and their pants down to their knees. The undertaker frowned. He was glad he was not in the police business. Dealing with nuts all the time! Cottrell's job was not one people usually coveted. Hell, even he had gotten into it by default, but it was probably the safest; dead people don't carry guns. Nor do they give you any backtalk or tell your secrets.

"I know this is difficult for you and I'm certainly sorry I have to question you about all these details. Are you sure you're up to talking to me now, Bill?" he asked in his smoothest tone, despite the thickening of his tongue from the vodka.

"Uh … sure. I guess so, John. Of course." The voice was faint, still a little foggy. Cottrell's heart went out to poor Bill Singleton, as much as he could feel sorry for anybody who created his own problems. He didn't like to say these things in public, but Bill was, to put it candidly, a jerk, a nerd, an incompetent. He was the type you felt sorry for, and, at the same time, you wanted to kick him in the ass because he didn't stand up for himself. He owned, of all things, an obscure little coin shop in town, and he didn't have many friends or know how to make them. The dumb bastard should have put his foot down, not let that girl work there alone at night. What was he, a man, or a mouse? But who was Cottrell to judge him there? Had he had any control over his own wife? He frowned.

"Bill," he continued, more slowly and with a touch of sympathy he didn't have to feign this time. "I need you to pick out something for Patsy Ann to wear, a dress she might wear to church or a suit with a nice blouse, something that always complimented your wife, something nice," he went on gently, "for the viewing."

Silence came through the receiver, and, for a moment, Cottrell thought the line went dead. "Bill—"

"Yes, I'm here," came the monotone in reply.

You *will* have a viewing, Bill? I mean ... there was no damage to her face, and except for the gunshot wound— "He stopped short, suddenly embarrassed. He was not usually so crass. What was he thinking?

"Bill," he said to the silence. "I would give my right arm if I didn't have to talk about any of this to you."

Cottrell waited a long time for a response. Finally, Bill stammered, "Uh ... uh, I don't know, John. I ... I haven't had time to think about the arrangements."

Cottrell decided to take the reins. It would have to be done. Bill was no help and their son, who lived a distance away, probably wouldn't arrive until tomorrow. "Just look into her closet, Bill," he said with the same soothing overtones he had carefully cultivated over the years, "and simply choose an outfit—something new, or something she's only worn a couple of times." He waited but there was no answer on the other end. "Bra, slip and panties—pantyhose too. No shoes," Cottrell reeled off, hoping Bill was writing it down. Still no response. After a while, he said, "Get one of Patsy's friends to help you with it if you have to, Bill. We'll do the rest, Margaret and me. And a recent photograph too, okay? Don't forget," he said. Margaret would often overdo the hair and makeup unless she had a picture of the deceased to copy. It was hard to get one of those pretty young beauticians to come in and work on dead bodies. Of course, Cottrell could understand why they wouldn't want to. He was lucky to get Margaret; she was old and nearsighted, but her penchant for always dressing in widow's black and saying the rosary beads during the visitation hours like a professional mourner was always a comfort to the families of the deceased.

"You can bring her things in anytime tomorrow, Bill," he heard himself say. "We'll talk about the viewing and the casket and all that when you come."

"Uh … Oh … Sure, John. I'll do that. I'll … Whatever you say, John. I'll be there."

"And don't forget to bring—"

"I know, I *know*! You told me what to bring!" Bill snapped and the receiver clicked in Cottrell's ear.

Singleton was an oddball, and the man *was* having a difficult time of it now, but as far as Cottrell was concerned, there was no excuse for being so damned rude. Singleton had been losing his wife slowly anyway;

everyone knew it except him. Cottrell didn't participate in gossip, except, of course, with Gene and that couldn't be considered gossip—it never went any further than the two of them sort of hashing out life, what sense they could make of it over the bottle of Absolut. He knew there had been plenty of gossip about his own wife and himself. Catherine had left him years ago, and for no better reason than she wanted to do her own thing, have a career—to pursue her art, such as it was. She learned sculpting at some adult ed class at the community college when the boys were all grown and away at school. And all of a sudden, with no warning that he was aware of, she went off to the University in Cincinnati—a woman in her fifties to pursue what? He couldn't fathom what! Even now. She wound up divorcing him, and he never heard of any art shows she was in or read her name in the papers. Men were losing control over women these days, Cottrell thought. "It's the times we live in," he said. He had the bad luck to be a victim of women's liberation. In his father's day, it never would have happened. Sad but true. Gene was sympathetic, but he was a priest—What did they know about women? Except for an occasional slip off the celibate ladder and, of course, what he learned second hand in the confessional. He wondered if Catherine, a Catholic herself, had confessed to Gene. But he knew Gene wouldn't tell him, even if she had, not so much because of the confession thing, but because it might hurt to know the truth. Suddenly he felt terribly sad for himself and for Bill Singleton, the coin dealer. Cottrell poured another shot, took off his glasses, cleaned them with the handkerchief from his pocket, and downed another shot; it felt good and hot going down. How many was that? He had lost count again. He put his size twelve feet up on the desk, leaned back in the swivel chair, and waited for the body to arrive.

When Bill came in, he would determine how much he could afford—that was harder with Bill than with other people. That dusty little shop couldn't make much of anything, but Bill was always quiet about what he earned, going off and making deals—out of town when he made them. These days eBay was probably killing what little business he had, and Bill was one of those in Cottrell's own generation who would have to be dragged kicking and screaming into the 21st Century if he got there at all. No, Bill would do business the old-fashioned way, without benefit of computers, and Cottrell bet if you counted the number of people that went into his store in the course of a month, there would be maybe four. People laughed about how Patsy supported him. She had a good job as a counselor at Pathright, Mazewood's center for psychiatric health. He supposed that Patsy's life insurance was minimal, whatever the company provided, and that wouldn't be a lot. At any rate, he would do his best to assist Bill in selecting something close to what Patsy Ann deserved to have.

Funny, he still remembered her playing out there

on the street, jumping rope in that pink skirt with the crinoline. Cottrell was maybe fifteen and Patsy five. Her parents, Andy and Bernice Pollack, had lived next door to the funeral parlor when his own father had owned it. Pollack, now a widower, retired and living in Florida, was in ill health; it would be all he could do to make it to the funeral. Bill and his father-in-law never got along in the past. It was a real shame. He couldn't fault Patsy for trying to bring them together, but Singleton never made enough money to suit Andrew Pollack, who had raised his only daughter to appreciate the finer things. Although the Pollacks had too much breeding to ever say so publicly, everyone knew Patsy had married beneath her.

4

Bill

American Heritage Coins in antique lettering was imprinted in red on the dusty glass window of Bill Singleton's shop. A blue and white sign, pasted across the middle and lower portion of the window, read "Baseball Cards." The inside was a tiny corner of an office, with an even smaller room curtained off in the back. Boxes of baseball cards and memorabilia he'd bought from a collector in Louisville last month were still stacked this way and that, either on chairs or on the window seat of the shop. He never seemed to have time to straighten them out, but he knew exactly where everything was when he was asked by a customer to produce a coin or card. There were two glass cases in the store where he kept special antique coins of silver and gold. He always carefully displayed the coins he knew were special, unique. The fact that he'd never been able to sell them did nothing to decrease their value to him. Someday a buyer who knew their true worth as well as Bill did would make an offer. In the meantime, the baseball cards were a new venture, and sometimes, if he got a good deal, he could make a small bundle that would last him for a while—but never long enough.

Bill opened the shop door with his key. The little store was located on First Street, just three blocks from his home. Home? That monstrosity? He still felt like a stranger there. The little house across the river in Abington, Ohio seemed more home to him than "Patsy's Pride" ever was. He had taken to calling it that behind her back—"Patsy's Pride." She was the one who wanted an old house with antiques in every room. She thought the Dutch colonial would be grand looking once they had finished the repairs and layered many coats of white over the now ugly red paint. Patsy had imagined it as regal as any of the older stately homes in Mazewood, so much more elegant than anything in Abington. Mazewood, Kentucky was a town full of old houses, many of which went back more than a hundred years—Patsy went on and on about Mazewood's Louisiana French and Dutch Colonial architecture. But to Bill, theirs was a monstrous old house that needed new plumbing and new wiring before one could even think about decorating, and God knows what else might go wrong every time you turned around. It took everything they both made to pay for the ugly dinosaur that she insisted on restoring to its original stature. In the meantime, he missed the house in Abington—the cramped brick ranch that, though crowded even for the three of them, made him remember where they had raised their young son. In Bill's mind, those were their happiest years. He had played ball with Allen in the backyard and Patsy had joined in sometimes too. The day they had picked up Bundy at the pet store was an especially important day; he and Allen had tossed a Frisbee around with the little black puppy chasing after it, and Patsy had laughed at them while she barbecued hamburgers. But the little house in Abington belonged to someone else, and now Patsy was gone too. His head ached and he became confused when he thought about it—the blood, his hands full of the crimson when he lifted her from the floor. It seemed like some surrealistic dream, like that strange painting above her desk—swirls. He couldn't think about it now. Allen would be flying in from California tomorrow. As much as he loved Allen, wanted to be with him now, Bill was glad it wasn't today; he needed some time alone—some space to think, to remember.

It was a Saturday and there wouldn't be many people around so early in the morning, only Fred at the Eat Shop down the street, and he would be busy in the back, preparing breakfast for a late-rising Saturday morning clientele; he would not open for at least another hour. Bill was glad of that too; he didn't want to talk to anyone, not the police, not Cottrell again, not any of his casual acquaintances. They would all be so sorry for him—he'd deal with that at the wake, not now. Entering the tiny room, Bill pulled the yellowed shades, not bothering to even yank the knotted string for illumination from the single light bulb overhead. He liked the cozy, too warm office; its small dark space was safe, comforting. And, over the years, he had explored every inch of it, found certain places in the back where he could hide some of the most valuable pieces, places that would never be discovered by any thief. His store had never been robbed in the thirty years he'd been there, but he didn't want to take the chance, he had always told Patsy. Now it didn't seem to matter at all if he were robbed. Or even killed. What could they take from him now? He had let his wife slip away from him. Somehow, he did not know how, he might have been able to prevent all of it happening. Bill removed a brick from the side wall in the curtained off section and reached inside to assure himself the valuables were still untouched.

Patsy had done research on all the old buildings in town, and this one dated back to the prohibition era; that was how he knew about the secret compartments. An article he had found in the library revealed that counterfeiters had once owned it as well. After searching and searching, tapping on walls for hollow places to find where they might have hidden their stacks of fake bills, he discovered only empty spaces, and never anything valuable except for a two-headed silver coin from the depression era. Removing it from the hiding hole, he dropped it into his pocket. This time when he replaced the brick, he smoothed on the quick drying spackle he'd brought from home. What was the use of hording treasures? His whole reason for living was gone.

Then he sat down on the straight-backed chair he'd reserved for an occasional customer, put his head in his hands and cried silently at first, the tears flowing down his cheeks and his body shaking. Finally, he sobbed in uninhibited grief, not caring whether Fred heard or not. He cried over the sounds of the large fans running to cool the hot ovens of the luncheonette. It was the first time Bill had shed tears since he had discovered his wife's body the night before. Aware of how totally alone he was, the coin dealer cried long and hard and loud. He knew the stores that sandwiched his shop in between them—Maine's Furniture Store and Henning's Paint and Wallpaper Emporium—were empty still and not a soul would listen to his pathetic sobbing. When there were no more tears in him, and he felt only the heavy pain in his chest that would lie there for a long, long time, he recreated in his mind the events of the previous night.

He remembered having awakened suddenly from a nap on the couch with a huge headache, his muscles aching from the hard surface underneath him. He didn't usually like sleeping on the primrose couch with wood trim Patsy had picked out for its antiquity, but he had been waiting for the phone to ring. He had been expecting a call from Patsy—to tell him she'd be working late and not to wait for her, that she'd grab a bite to eat at Hardees. Having arrived home at six, he had found the house cold and quiet, without any of the warmth and light that Patsy's presence gave it when she was already there and cooking dinner. Once again, he tried to come to terms with the fact that his wife was still at work, putting in extra time. And primarily because she was the major breadwinner lately, she had reminded him only too often. He had not been able to make a deal for a long time, let alone a "sweet deal" that would keep him on easy street for a while. His luck waning for never having the most desirable coins, he had recently gotten into the baseball card thing, but too late—the market for memorabilia, though steady for a while, was dying out. Time and again his wife brought that up and nudged the old sore in his side. But he would always forgive her.

So, why hadn't there been a call? Perhaps he hadn't heard the phone, slept through its ringing; he had done that before when he was very, very tired. Bill retraced the events prior to his falling asleep. The last he remembered it was six o'clock when he lay on the couch and closed his eyes. The clock read eleven now. He must have slept soundly. The house was still, quiet and dark, eerie even. A dread he couldn't fathom the reason for began to fill him with anxiety. Just to reassure himself she was not there, Bill checked every room, switching on the lights, hoping to find Patsy curled up and asleep in one of the bedrooms, an afghan covering her. She was often too tired to take off anything but her shoes when she'd come home so late. The gloominess of the house with its tall antiques looking down at him from every corner in the semi-darkness oppressed him severely—a 19th century hat rack with scrolling in its heavy dark wood reminded him of a Dracula character. He switched on all the lights. "To hell with the electricity bill," he said. He called to the black lab, and Bundy slowly got up from his niche by the fireplace and waddled over to his master to receive a pat on the head. "Where's the mistress of the house, old Bun?" Bill queried the dog, rubbing him behind the ears. Then he picked up the phone in the kitchen and began dialing. Bundy wagged his tail slowly and whimpered as an old dog is prone to doing, with less insistence than when he was a young pup. "I'll take you out soon, I promise," he told Bundy, patting him again as he listened to the ringing on the other end. No answer.

He ran all the way—all nine blocks to the Center. To offset the money the house was sucking from their budget, the Singletons kept only one car now—a '99 yellow Cadillac that Patsy drove to work. She would need it for an occasional lunch date or to visit one of Pathright's satellite offices, and what did he need it for? A trip across the bridge to Ohio once in a while, where he would sit and gaze back at Mazewood from the other side of the river, from the town of Abington; there he would eat his lunch from a paper bag. Sometimes he would even park near the house where they used to live and he would remember how it was then, though sometimes his memory was distorted and he could not recall exactly, but he loved to remember those early days, when he was happiest.

Panting so hard, he felt a pain in his chest, Bill stopped momentarily to regain his wind. His hand rested on the iron railing that led up the back steps of the building. When was he going to learn he couldn't run like a youngster anymore? His body had gotten wider, heavier. He reminded himself he was nearly fifty. His breath came rapidly, so rapidly he thought he was hyperventilating. But after a few moments, he was calm again.

Bill tapped a rhythmic pattern on the door, the way he always did, and waited for Patsy to let him inside. He could see the light burning in her office; he knew she was there. Her car was the only one in the lot. More and more she had been working overtime—an appointment didn't show up until late, and rather than rearrange it or disappoint someone, Patsy stayed. Sometimes she even stayed to do paperwork that had piled up high on her desk. And later he would walk there to meet her and drive her home—on good days, when her supervisor Charlie Sweet was not there. Sweet was the psychologist on staff who would offer to drive her home, assuring she arrived at the house on Market Street and inside the door safely. It irritated Bill more and more—Charlie Sweet and the late nights! He said his name again emphasizing the "sweet" sarcastically. It gave him satisfaction to pronounce it that way. He couldn't argue that Patsy should not work so much when she countered that they needed her overtime salary to make ends meet. She was running therapy sessions on Saturdays now that she had passed all the necessary exams and was qualified to do so. And all to pay for that dinosaur of a house. When Patsy had gone back to college, they had both agreed that the money she could make would make their life a lot easier, but he had not expected the rift, the chasm that had developed between the two of them because of it—he pondered how much Patsy had changed, yet he could not logically fault her for anything. She had done everything right; she had the best of motives. But Patsy's attitude, even her vocabulary, had changed. With a start, Bill realized he did not know this new woman.

He tapped on the door of the counseling center again, waited, and then tapped louder. Still no sound. He put his hand on the doorknob expecting it to be locked, but to his surprise it flung open. Her office door was closed. He heard his heart pound in his ears, a deafening sound. He pushed on the door hard, as hard as he could, but something heavy blocked it. Some sort of clump lay behind the door.

Funny how the red polka dots on the white dress camouflaged the bullet hole at first; it looked like just one more polka dot, only larger than the rest. He could only think how odd she looked there on the floor, like some stranger, not like Patsy at all. Those brightly colored clothes she'd taken to buying lately were not *her* ... not the way he wanted to remember her. Even the office looked different. She had replaced the painting of an Irish cottage, usually on the wall behind her desk, with some garishly painted he did not know what—it was weird what passed for art. Maybe it was something that Charlie Sweet had decided should go there.

For the viewing he selected a sedate navy granny style dress with a white collar and demure little pink and white flowers. He discarded the dresses she had bought in the last few months—the lacy white "off the shoulder" one and the red spaghetti strapped one, putting them in a bag for the Goodwill—something had come over her, some temporary insanity had suddenly obsessed her. It embarrassed him that Allen, or even one of the neighbors, might look in her closet and find the whorish clothing there. The police probably will have to keep the polka dot one. He regretted that. Those clothes were *not* Patsy; they belonged to someone else, someone he didn't know.

5

Les

"And what did you do then?" Detective Reese asked, his eyes on Singleton. Suddenly he wondered if he shouldn't have insisted that Bill come down to the station house, or even taken him in last night for questioning; it was, after all, standard procedure. But Bill had not come into the police station on his own, so it was nearly noon before Lester, along with another policeman, went to the Singleton house to investigate the murder. He would have to go to Patsy Singleton's residence to further the investigation anyway, though he doubted a warrant would be necessary for a search.

"I'll repeat the question," Reese said a little louder when Bill didn't answer. "What did you do then?"

"I-I-d-d-don't know exactly," Bill stuttered. "I went to her, felt for a pulse." He looked down at his clothes, as if he expected to see the blood stains still there, but he had evidently showered and changed, though his clothes looked as if he'd slept in them. Bill's dog brown eyes drooped when he looked into Les's eyes. But there were no tears. Maybe he's cried himself out already, Les thought.

"It … the pulse that is, was so faint I didn't know for sure if she was still alive. Her hands were cold—so terribly cold." He began to tremble. "I think I just held her there for—for I don't know how long. Then I guess that's when I called an ambulance." His sad eyes seemed to plead with the detective to halt the questioning, to let him mourn. Reese wondered if this poor, broken man had murdered his wife.

Reese had been up all night with the investigation and called Rosemarie early that morning from the station. His wife's emotions overwhelmed her, ruled her. She could not imagine that anyone could kill such a sweet lady like Patricia Singleton, the sole supporter of Rosie's art.

Twenty years of police work had taught Reese not to let pity interfere with his work. Though he couldn't help feeling sympathy for Singleton, he pressed on. "We are questioning others too, Bill. I am not trying to make it hard on you, but now, with the details fresh in your mind, is the best time—"

"I might as well have been the one to pull the trigger," Bill said, his beagle eyes sincere and pathetic. He had been sitting down on the couch, but now he rose in an agitated state, grabbing Reese's arm. "I shouldn't have insisted she protect herself. But how was I to know that … I-I just worried so about her, Lester," he said. Letting go of Reese's sport jacket, apparently embarrassed at his sudden burst of emotion, Bill tried to explain. "I just worried so about her," he repeated, his voice quieter now. "Do you see how I was so worried about her?"

Reese looked down at the highly polished parquet floor to avoid the eyes of the confessor again. The thought that popped into his head was that Patsy certainly was a "house proud" woman—he couldn't imagine Bill caring that much about floors. Enough to buff them to this high polished state.

"Well, aren't I?" he asked Reese.

"Aren't you what?" Reese said.

"Aren't I *responsible*?" Bill Singleton demanded of the detective.

Reese looked up at him. The suspect, if that's what he was, was trembling like a deer trapped by headlights.

"Are you saying that you killed her, Bill?" The coin dealer was pathetic in his helplessness, a wrinkled mass, a broken man. Reese tried to imagine some sort of accident, a gun going off in a scuffle. After all, Bill didn't have a real alibi and they had not come up with any witnesses.

"No, no, no," Bill said, an impatience overtaking him. "You don't understand … I couldn't hurt Patsy. I loved her," he said, his voice breaking again. He took out a silver coin from his pocket and nervously turned it over and over; looking at it as if it might suddenly give him the words he needed to explain.

The thought occurred to Reese that perhaps the hospital had released Singleton prematurely, that he was still in shock. "Where is the gun, Bill?"

Bill looked at Resse as if he were from another planet. "The murderer has it, of course."

The detective, wearing what he knew was a deadpan expression, waited for the coin dealer to continue.

"I gave her a gun to keep in the office," he said. "I shouldn't have. Now I know I shouldn't have even taught her how to use it—as much as I knew how … I'm not much with a gun either—at the range over in Ohio. She got pretty good at it too," Bill said with an odd pride— better shot than I ever was. The truth is I really detest guns, Lester. Hate them, as a matter of fact. Except of course as antiquity, like the coins. But, in this day and age, well, a person needs protection, don't they? Particularly a woman. Patsy needed protection, didn't she?"

"Go on." Reese said, "tell me more about the gun. What did she do with it?"

He sat down in a wing-backed chair by the fireplace where the old dog lay. One eye opened and closed but that was the only movement in the animal since Reese and Officer Kessler had arrived. "She kept it in her desk drawer," he said, "I asked her to, and she did it. Nobody else knew, not even her co-workers or Charlie. At least that's what she told me. He would have never gone for it, she said. It was against regulations anyway—to have a gun on the premises. She and I were the only ones who knew about it." Singleton got up from the chair in the living room and paced back and forth, his hands in the pockets of his rumpled beige trousers. Again, he stared at the coin, turning it over and over. Reese watched him. The coin dealer wore a beige golf shirt, as rumpled and sweaty as the pants, but there were no blood stains.

It was warm in the house and Detective Reese shed his summer blazer. A white long-sleeved shirt, which he continually wore, showed perspiration rings under the arms.

Singleton seemed suddenly aware of the oppressive heat, apologized excessively for the absence of any air conditioning. The house was still undergoing renovation and central air was the next thing Patsy had had on the agenda, he told Reese. A ceiling fan whirred loudly above them, but it had little effect in the large room.

"Hey, Lester! Come up here, Lester!" The urgency in Officer Kessler's voice interrupted the hypnotic noises of the fan and the detective's thoughts.

"What is it, Jerome?" Reese yelled upstairs, still watching Patsy's husband turn the coin again and again in his palm without looking at it. He finally put the piece of silver back in his pocket and sighed. "It'll cost a fortune to cool this place," Bill Singleton said, shaking his head.

"Something up here you better take a look at, sir," Kessler replied.

Lester had wanted to come prepared with a search warrant, a search meant to be cursory at best; but it was routine as far as he was concerned and saved time in the long run. But the judge had been angry when Reese called him early that morning for the documentation. "You're back in Mazewood, Reese," he had said angrily. Not in the city! We make our own rules here!"

Bill didn't seem to mind or even consider that he might be a *real* suspect, that is not beyond the guilt he was imposing upon himself by insisting Patsy have a means of protecting herself from harm. But Reese could not discount any possibility yet. The facts were that Mrs. Patsy Singleton had died at two a.m. Saturday morning of a gunshot wound inflicted by a .22 bullet from a handgun sometime between eight and ten Friday evening. No weapon had yet been found so it was probably not a suicide. And the corner's determination confirmed this by providing a report of the trajectory of the bullet and the distance from which it was fired. Singleton was found on the scene when the medics and police arrived at about the same time. The police only had Bill's word for how long he had been there. No witnesses had come forward. One or two people thought they had heard what sounded like a car backfiring around eight thirty or so but paid little attention to it.

Reese bounded up the steps to find his assistant in the master bedroom. The officer pointed out a gun cabinet. "Look at what I found! Not a bad collection of rifles and shot guns here. And look at this, Lester," Kessler said. He took out a box at the bottom of the cabinet. There was a molding for a gun, even a description of it on the side of the box. "It's for a .22 handgun. A Smith and Wesson. The receipt's still here. Got it from a place in Virginia, mail order."

"I deal in guns sometimes too, usually old ones, mostly for show," Bill said quietly. "And I told you, I bought that one for Patsy."

Lester turned and looked at Bill, who had followed him upstairs and now stood waiting at the doorway while he and Kessler examined the rest of the gun cabinet.

Bill paid little attention to them, as if what they were concerned with was no concern of his. He sat down on the bed.

Reese examined the guns and found that what Bill said was true. Most of them were antique replicas, except for the one that was missing. He glanced again at Bill, inviting more explanation.

"I *gave* her a gun, Lester. I told you that. It was small enough for her to handle and keep inside a drawer under her desk."

"*This* gun, Bill?" He indicated the box.

Bill nodded.

"So where is it? Was it in her desk last night?"

"I don't know. It was gone when I got there, I guess. I don't know. I didn't look in the drawer. Why don't you check her appointment book? You've already searched my house and my office and obviously it's not here."

"Check the rest of the house again, Jerome, and let

me know if you find anything at all."

"Right, sir." The sergeant left while Reese sat down beside the widower, who was now stretched out on the bed with his hands at his sides, staring at the ceiling. His lips quivered a little as if he might cry. He seemed as if he wanted to talk but was having difficulty. Reese could hear Kessler downstairs, combing the house thoroughly now, thinking he'll find that gun, but Lester knew it wasn't there. He prodded further. "OK, we'll check out every one of the clients *and* Patsy's co-workers—anybody who might have seen her that day. We've already begun that part of the investigation. Her last appointment was a Wendell Troy. You know him?"

Singleton didn't answer right away. A few moments passed before he said, "Yeah, I know him, Lester. I warned her about him. He's the kind with the earring and the tattoo and the drug habit. Patsy always thought she could help that kind of people. But you know what?" He looked over at the detective and said," You can't help them, Lester. They been raised all wrong, and they're too far gone."

"We'll check him out, Bill."

Bill nodded. "You do that," he said.

"But, in the meantime, you're the last one to have seen your wife alive, as far as we know. You'd better tell me absolutely everything."

"It's that crazy Troy must have done it, Lester. Wendell Troy. He's the one," Bill said, his voice quivering. "I know he did it. If you don't get him, *I* will!" The sudden anger in Singleton's voice seemed strange coming from such a mild-mannered man. Lester had known him since they were kids in public school, though he hadn't had much contact in the years he'd been with the Chicago Police Department. He'd come home and visit his mother and then be off again—never enough time to spend at home or with people he'd not seen in years. His mother had complained about that, and he was her only son. And after she died, there was just no reason to come back really. It was just a turn of fate, his marriage to Rosemarie Marquez that caused him to change his attitude, to want to raise his sons in a relatively crime-free small town where some people still knew him. Singleton had gone to high school here in Mazewood and had begun a business shortly after his marriage to Patsy. Reese had not known Patsy growing up, except as one of the quiet little Catholic school girls, four years younger and of little importance to them when they were in high school. Bill was never part of his crowd though. He was always polite, gentle to a fault—even a little too mild mannered. Meek was a better word, Reese thought, and adulthood hadn't changed him much. His wife had been playing around on him for some time if one believed the rumors—Charlie Sweet had reluctantly admitted to Reese just that morning what the whole town knew. No doubt Charlie was the reason why she had stayed late most nights, but the psychologist had an airtight alibi for the time in question on the night of the murder—quite a few of his friends—upstanding members of the community—were at his house for dinner. He and his wife kept up appearances for the public, even though they were always on the verge of a divorce. Dr. Sweet admitted to Reese that he and Patsy had had a brief affair, but he told Reese that it had suddenly ended. It hadn't lasted long, he said, maybe a month or two—then it was over. She had been the one to end it, saying it was a mistake. Sweet was relieved. It had gotten in the way of their professional lives and, according to him, they had simply returned to being just good friends and colleagues with no bitterness on either side. That, of course, was Sweet's version, thought Reese. So far, there was no corroboration and Patsy couldn't testify to that amicable agreement.

"Did you question that Dr. Sweet about the murder?" Bill asked. "He worked late a lot of times—and he'd often still be there when I picked up Patsy—maybe he knows where the gun is. His voice rose when he said, "Maybe *he's* the one who did it!"

"The psychologist and I talked this morning," Reese said.

"And?"

"He had no knowledge of it, he said. He left the center around 3:00 in the afternoon. And witnesses put him at his home during the murder."

Bill inhaled deeply and blew it out in jagged breaths.

He was so silent after that that Reese looked at him to see if he'd fallen asleep. Finally, he spoke. "I don't trust that damned Charlie Sweet character as far as I can throw him. That Wendell Troy neither."

Reese let the remark go without comment.

" Patsy and I talked about everything—just everything. I know what she felt about that young Troy fellow," Bill said. "Good looking, long blonde hair, dresses like a refugee from a Salvation Army store, for Pete's sake. I could just tell that he was after her—that kind always are. What could she expect anyway? Did I tell you he wears a gold earring—on the left ear I think…? I warned her. I told her he was not the misunderstood kid she thought he was. That he was dangerous." He was sitting up now on the edge of the bed, staring at his dusty, black wingtip shoes. He took a handkerchief out of his pocket and wiped the minute flakes of dust off the shoes in a careful back-and-forth motion.

Reese thought about the dust on the windows of the coin shop. "How strong were her feelings for him—Troy, I mean?" he asked. Then, embarrassed for Bill, he rephrased the question: "I mean, what else did she say about this Wendell Troy?" His voice was barely above a whisper now and strangely hoarse, as if he were having trouble broaching the subject.

Bill snarled. "He was a *good* boy underneath," she would always say. "She was so naive in that way, Lester, believing everybody. You'd think after all those courses in psychology she'd know about the evil, wouldn't you?"

Reese didn't answer, letting him talk.

"Not that Patsy believed she was in danger; she was just placating me, making me feel better by keeping the gun in her desk. It was no doubt Troy who found out she had the gun and turned it on her. Murdered her. I'm sure of it." Bill's anger was escalating as his voice rose. "Why are you wasting time here? Why don't you go after my wife's murderer?" Finally, he looked away from Reese and began staring at the floor. His forearms rested on his thighs and his head hung down near his knees. He seemed exhausted from the outburst and when he finally did speak, it was with quiet resignation. "If you want to arrest me too, go ahead, Lester," he said with remorse; "I'm just as guilty as that boy Troy. I should have been more firm with my wife, protected her from this. She liked to think she was a modern woman, but she was really a sweet old-fashioned girl, delicate is the word. I should have protected her."

"What could you have done, Bill?"

There was no answer. After a long silence, Reese said, "We'll bring Troy in for questioning." And for another moment he just sat there beside the man on the bed, studying the pattern of tiny blue roses on the bedspread and thinking how much the entire room reflected what he knew of Patsy Singleton's personality; from the antique coverlet to the baroque frames on the wall, it was all *her* taste, her *house*. Except that her penchant for modern art had obviously begun to emerge. He had recognized his own wife's lightening strokes of color above the body of the deceased when he first entered the crime scene at Patsy's office. It was shocking at first, and now, after seeing the rest of her possessions, it seemed even more of an anomaly. What was it Rosie had said that occurred to him now? ... something about how the traditional and the avant garde can exist alongside one another juxtaposed in the same painting, or even the same person.... He wondered if it were true, or just some of the philosophies according to Rosemarie Reese. Rosie was often insightful, and she knew a lot about art, but police work had taught him to mistrust the pieces that do not fit.

The detective scrutinized the other man's profile. Singleton's eyes were now closed but his jaw was set and his lips tight. Reese read pain in the widower's pallid complexion; it was a face that had aged years, even in the last few hours. Reese found it tough to say what he knew was necessary. "Listen, Singleton," he began sharply, as if his mere will could bring the man out of his grief. Then feeling foolish and unnecessarily harsh, he spoke again, quickly but with as much compassion as he knew how: "Bill ... I know this is a bad time to bring this up, but there's no avoiding it. I have to ask you something: Did you know your wife had been having an affair?"

6

Gene

Father Wallace sat reading his breviary at the breakfast table when the monsignor walked in. "You look like hell, Gene." The bulbous, bald-headed man was unnecessarily cheerful when he sat down beside his assistant pastor. He picked up the freshly laundered napkin, daintily laid it in his lap, and downed his glass of orange juice already on the table. Gene often saved his orange juice for last or ignored it altogether—that was the difference between them—Monsignor Edward Ahearn played the game, no matter what it was, according to the rules, right down to orange juice first. He bent rules, sure, but only when it was to his own advantage.

Father Wallace didn't answer or even look up from his prayers; his eyes sped over the black and white. He saw the words and then there was Patsy Singleton's face popping up in front of him, unbidden but inevitable. He sighed and began again, willing the words. A pajama sleeve peeked out from under the wider black sleeve of his cassock; he hadn't had time to change that morning before he went to the hospital to give communion to Mrs. Cartwright and to that young kid Steven, who was still showing no signs of recovery no matter how much chemotherapy they blasted him with. Now he admonished himself for squirming under the pastor's scrutiny. He admonished himself for his grief. He had no right to it. Who did he think he was anyway? He read; he tried to pray.

"If you didn't stay up half the night drinking with that friend of yours at the funeral parlor, you'd be able to get up with enough time before mass to take care of your priestly obligations."

Gene tried to ignore Monsignor Ahearn, to wait patiently for him to say his piece while he attempted to steady his trembling hands by gripping the leather-bound edges of his breviary. And there she was again. Sweet Patsy. Then her life ebbing out as he gave her last rites. He was the last one to hold her, he thought. How could she be dead? How could this have happened?

"That's probably why you haven't advanced further than an assistant pastor at your age. How old are you now, Gene? Fifty-five?" The monsignor chortled. "Something wrong with a man your age who hasn't risen above an assistant's position in a small town."

He wasn't going to let it be, so Father Wallace sighed and reluctantly looked up from the words he knew by heart anyway. "Edward, when was the last time you answered the door to hear a confession in the middle of the week? In the middle of the night? Stayed all night with a bereaved family? Or even said the rosary at the funeral home?"

"I say mass every morning at 8:00 a.m. as I'm scheduled to do. People can count on me, Gene, on my systematic regularity. It's a hallmark of my—"

Gene raised his index finger, interrupting. "But just remember," he said, "I'm taking over Patsy Singleton's funeral … "He felt light-headed when he said her name, but he went on, "… the one you begged off. I know the only reason is that it interrupts that tidy schedule of yours, not to mention the fact that you can't deal with grief. It's messy isn't it, Edward. Sin is messy. Emotion is messy."

Monsignor Ahearn held up his palms, conceding. "All right, all right. Don't get so testy. That's what rubbing elbows with the poor parishioners gets you. All that emotion! It's so peasant-like."

Gene frowned…. He really did hate the man, God forgive him.

"If you act like you're a cut above them," Ahearn continued, "you'll get more respect. Believe me, Gene. I know what I'm talking about. Everybody's gossiping about your battle with booze. You're a joke in this town. It's getting to be embarrassing."

"Don't ride me about what I do in my spare time, Edward," Gene said, gritting his teeth. "I take care of what I've been assigned, don't I? More even. And I'm sober when I have to be." He opened the breviary again and pretended to pray by moving his lips, but the woman's face returned as he moved them. "Patsy ... Dear Patsy," he whispered and hoped Ahearn hadn't heard. He remembered her laugh, her teasing look. And what happened between them that he should have been strong enough to avoid. But *could* he have? Even though he wanted to let her go, end it, could he really have done it finally, or would he have left the vocation he believed in and loved more than anything else in the world? He may have had his doubts in the past, but he was a priest, first and always, and when he had tried to tell her ... waited for her ... Then the hospital. "Dear Patsy," his lips mouthed. The Lord had seen fit to save his vocation but had taken her from him.

Ahearn was silent until the assistant's lips had quit moving. "That's your whole trouble, you know, Gene. Your *indiscretion*. Don't let your vices show so much to the little people."

Gene looked up, momentarily startled, tears glistening in his eyes.

The monsignor smiled. His row of white. gleaming teeth irritated Gene even more than his healthy-looking rosy cheeks. He was nothing more than a lousy politician—a showman. A disgrace to what priesthood was supposed to be.... But was he, Eugene Wallace, any better? On good days he thought he was. But this was not a good day.

Ahearn would not stop, even though Father Wallace had lowered his head again, and this time farther over his breviary. "Why don't you put the hospital visits on that young seminarian who comes in once a week," he suggested in a patronizing tone. "What's his name? Howard or something."

Gene raised his head to reply but the stream of light coming in the kitchen window, rather like a heavenly stream reflecting on the pastor's bald head, arrested his attention for a moment. "Harold," he said, when he remembered what the monsignor had asked.

"What?"

"The seminarian's name is Harold Fine," Gene answered absently, still gazing at the light with its tiny dust specks in the ray that shone upon the pastor's head. Like an El Greco painting, he mused. Then Gene almost felt like laughing at the absurdity. El Greco's figures were long, thin, and suffering creatures, reaching toward heaven in their religiosity. Ahearn's figure was far from lean, sacrificial, and except in hypocrisy, his soul didn't reach that often toward heaven. But whose did? Certainly not his own.

"Well, whatever his name is," Ahearn said, dismissing his error with a wave of his hand as if it were of as little importance as one of those specks of dust in God's light. "Let me give you some advice," he said. "If you'd let Harold do some of your routine work, you'd be able to go to the conference next weekend if you really wanted to—hobnob with the bishop and the boys in Covington," he said playfully, and winking too, as if they shared some dirty secret between them. Gene was disgusted. "You'd be amazed at what a little politics can accomplish for a career," the monsignor advised.

"The conference is hogwash, and we all know the diocese gives out promotions to pastors who bleed their congregations dry—you know it and I know it. Don't be a goddamned hypocrite in front of me, Edward. I am not one of your poor parishioners, nor am I your kind of priest." He set down the breviary beside his plate and, elbows bent on the table, headache throbbing, buried his face in his hands. He truly didn't know what kind of a priest he was, but he understood that Ahearn was his punishment. God forgive me, he prayed.

Father Wallace was grateful for the silence that followed when the other priest turned and walked indignantly from the room, but not without his final say: "The booze will be the death of you, Gene. Even if it were not a sin—it's not going to solve any of your problems, you know. And it'll get you in the end."

He knew Edward Ahearn would never let him have the last word, so he bit his lip until he drew blood rather than reply.

★★★

In the sacristy, while he put on his vestments, the priest tried not to think about it, tried to keep the image of Patsy out of his mind—Patsy living, Patsy with the life bled out of her when he administered last rights—he, her priest. Then he kept recalling the strange confession again and again, almost word for word—If he *could* talk about it, John Cottrell would be the one he'd tell. Maybe he *should* confess it—all of it. Certainly not to Monsignor Ahearn. He wouldn't confess so much as a venial sin to that hypocritical old son of a bitch. He had never talked to Cottrell about a confession that he remembered, at least he hoped he hadn't; but sometimes there were blanks in his memory, gaps where he couldn't remember what he had said or done. Once he had awakened still in his car with his station wagon parked half on and half off the sidewalk. Luckily no one had seen him, and he had sneaked into the rectory and tiptoed upstairs before the housekeeper Elsie arrived and before Edward was up. But that was before Patsy, before he had stopped the drinking, well, almost.

"Father … Father!" The altar boy was tugging at his sleeve. "They're waiting for us, Father. It's time."

When he finally allowed himself to think beyond having to talk about Patsy—he did it as if it were someone else he were talking about, as if it were Bill's wife and not the *real* Patsy—he placed his mind on the ritual and what was to come next to get through the mass before he allowed his eyes to scan the faces of the small group behind the pallbearers at the funeral. Wallace saw the familiar face, the one he had seen week after week with the same expression. He could detect nothing of the remorse he had been privy to in the confessional. And then, later, at the chapel in the cemetery, he saw only painful loss on all their faces; the confessor, Patsy's co-workers, her friends, and everyone else—the worst kind of loss for each of them. There were people who had been her clients, some he knew, and some he didn't. Old-timers who'd known the family for years, Patsy's parents, their son Allen. He wondered if he had really heard the confession at all. But this was not some kind of illusion or mirage brought on by the alcohol he had consumed when he had finally left Patsy—on Saturday morning he had slid open the door to the confessional booth on the right, the one that always made the creaky sound. A recognizable monotone of the confessor's voice never wavered, told what he had done, answered all his questions in a matter-of-fact tone, regardless of what the priest wanted to know. With an apparently sincere act of contrition the penitent swore before God, agreed to make what restitution that could be offered, suffer for the sin—and that meant telling the police, of course. He had promised before him and before God. Priest and penitent prayed for Patsy Ann Singleton's soul, for their souls and the souls of the faithful departed, for everyone involved. The sinner, truly sorry, had returned to the fold. And Gene, despite his anger, despite his rage at the sinner, at the act and the senseless loss of Patsy Ann Singleton, had cried for both of them—and himself.

… But now? What now? …

He hoped Patsy had made a good act of contrition before expiring, that she had had time to set things right, but she was unconscious when he laid his hands on her body and she expired shortly thereafter. Patsy had not come to church with Bill for some time. He remembered the time he'd seen her—at the Speedway—that moment had started it all for him. They were both paying for gas. She seemed embarrassed. He didn't know why.

"Oh, hello, Father," she said. She was wearing that red and white polka dot dress, the one that she had died in, and her face flushed the color of the dots. Her smile dazzled him. It was as if he were seeing her for the very first time.

"It's nice to see you, Patsy," Gene said. "Bill tells me you've been rather busy these days."

"Why, yes, Father. I … uh, I've had a lot of cases—"

"Patsy," he said, looking into her eyes, brown pools of passion—he was no fool. He recognized it. "Don't stay away too long." With that he turned to pick up his change from the register, raised a hand in a parting gesture, and left her, he imagined, staring after him. He had known about her affair with Charlie, nearly everyone in the town knew, and the only one who didn't was her husband. Or perhaps Bill found it too difficult to admit.

"Father?" she called to him before she got in her car

"Yes," he replied, turning.

"Could I come and see you sometime—at the rectory?"

"Of course," he said. He was aware of how casual he looked without his Roman collar and wondered if she saw him differently. He was wearing one of those golf shirts, a yellow one, and pair of brown slacks. They never met at the rectory. It had begun at the grotto fountain behind the convent when the nuns were gone for the summer, and no one was around. Patsy liked it there. He had found her there one day when he took a short cut into the sacristy—perhaps she had been at prayer, he didn't know. They began to talk, began to have lunch there on occasion ... and then they had gone to see a play in Cincinnati, a musical—he drove in his car, she in hers ... they met at the theatre ... after that ... God saw fit to take her away from him after he had made the decision to give her up. For Bill. For God. For the sake of something more important than themselves, he reasoned. He once remembered someone saying that irony is, after all, simply God's sense of humor. It must be true, he thought.

Gene sighed heavily. He put his head down on his desk, hoping the throbbing ache would leave him. He had taken to having his meals in the study while he worked; the paperwork had begun to get out of control. Ahearn had been recently promoted and would soon be leaving theirs for a larger parish, so it was up to him to take over until a new pastor could be appointed. The myriad of numbers was not his forte but his motive for delving into them so soon was simply to be left alone; Ahearn always seemed to be able to read the inner struggle from his face—he was that transparent—and he didn't want to be subjected to the probing. Besides, he needed time. He knew where his duty began, but he didn't know for sure where it ended. The rules were clear certainly. Though he'd twisted and stretched rules before with little regret, justifying his actions with the circumstances, he had never intentionally broken the seal of the confessional. He had tried to talk to Bill alone about where his duty lay, but with little result. Though a non-Catholic and not an especially good friend of Bill or Patsy Singleton, Detective Reese attended the funeral, watching the ritual in his cold, calculating way, listening to Gene's eulogy with interest. He wondered if the detective could read his guilt, his pain, the slight trembling in his voice, his flushed face, or if the Roman collar and purple vestments were distracting enough to keep the man's eyes from his face. Reese scanned the friends and relatives with piercing eyes of someone who sought nothing but truth, any kind of truth. Hard and cold truth. Gene found it difficult to look at the man. He hurried back after the prayers at the funeral, hid away in his study, and waited for the confessor to make restitution for his sins, knowing that after all this time had passed, he wasn't going to do so. Gene had given the absolution in good faith. He was not responsible for turning the murderer in to the police.

"Father Wallace," the housekeeper said, knocking loudly. He hadn't heard her the first time she'd rapped at the door. "There's a man here to see you."

"Who is it, Elsie? I'm busy here," he told her as she poked her head in the door, and he began rousing himself from his reverie.

"I don't know who 'tis for sure, Father, but I think he said he's with the police," she whispered, frightened. But he's not wearing a uniform," she said in her nervous flittering voice. She looked at the priest curiously, waiting for him to explain it or tell her what to do...

Father Wallace's heart skipped a beat. So soon? He had expected there might be visit from the detective, but he was not ready.

"What should I tell him, Father?" She was becoming agitated now. So much indecision unnerved her. Ahearn complained about her constantly, wanted to hire another housekeeper, but Elsie needed to work, or she'd be worse. If he didn't go out to greet his guest, she would become hysterical and start screaming, maybe even throwing things about the rectory. Elsie Malone was diagnosed with schizophrenia and a patient on whom the new miracle medicines had no effect; she'd never get employment anywhere else, and Wallace knew it. He would fight to the death for her to keep this job. But for now, he'd have to tell her something.

"Can you find out what he wants, Elsie?" He would stall the detective for time. Time to think. Think, he told himself as he paced the office. First, he would find out how much the detective knew—or if it were only his suspicions that brought him here. Could he have heard about the confession? But how? Not under any circumstances could he talk about a confession. No, he could not, *would* not break the seal.

In a moment Elsie had returned and Gene met her at the door. "Says it's about the Patsy Singleton murder, Father," she whispered. "What on earth?" she exclaimed with large questioning, waterless eyes, her withered hand to her mouth. "What do you suppose he's come *here* for?"

In a moment he was there, behind Elsie. "Detective Lester Reese, Mazewood Police Department," he said, holding out his hand to the priest when Elsie had turned and skittered back into the kitchen.

"Gene Wallace," the priest answered, shaking the firm hand. "Well, what can I do for you, Detective? I don't believe you're one of our parishioners?" Or is this a pleasant surprise and you're here to convert to Catholicism?" he joked, smiling.

Reese laughed, but there was a dead seriousness in his eyes. "No, my wife Rosemarie is a Catholic, Father, but she's not religious. That is, she believes in God and the saints and all that, I think, but she doesn't go to church."

"I see," the priest said with a smile. The detective's eyes were a light green, icy and hard as marbles, the way he imagined an iceberg that took on the color of the ocean would look. Gene would dance around his questions, spar with him, but he would not give him what he wanted.

7

Cottrell

"Won't you come in Detective Reese," Cottrell said.

Reese took off his hat and entered the vestibule of the funeral home.

"To what do I owe this visit, Detective? Has there been a death in your family?"

"No, sir, but it is official business. My business, rather than yours."

Cottrell led the detective to the back of the house where his office was located, past the room with the empty caskets, a room where the French doors remained open when there was no funeral in progress. "I have a fine selection of caskets here, Detective, if you ever have the need." He continued walking when the visitor didn't answer.

Cottrell pointed to a chair in front of his cherry desk and then sat behind it, his large hands spread out over the sooth surface, as if he were about to propose the subject, not Reese. "So, what can I do for you, Detective?" he said.

"Patsy Ann Singleton's murder," Reese said flatly.

Cottrell shook his head. "Poor Patsy Ann," he said. It was such a sad funeral. And poor Bill. I never felt as sorry for any human being as I did him."

Reese lowered his eyes but didn't commiserate.

"So why are you coming here, Detective?" Cottrell said. "What information can I give you that you don't have already? It's been weeks."

Reese sighed. "I know you know who did it."

"Me?" Cottrell feigned surprise. "You are the policeman. I'm just an undertaker. Why would I know who murdered Patsy Singleton?" He had heard that Lester Reese was such a dogged policeman, took pride in his investigations and the fact that he'd solved just about every case he'd ever been involved in in Chicago. It was no wonder he was still actively seeking her killer.

"Didn't they arrest that Wendell Troy fellow? The kid who was Patsy's patient?"

"We got him on drug charges, that's all."

"Did you ever get a confession?"

"No," Reese said. "He didn't do it."

"He's got an alibi, I guess?" Cottrell asked. He stopped himself from asking who Reese suspected.

"No, he doesn't really. But he didn't do it."

"You don't say?"

"No, Cottrell. He's not guilty."

"Whatever do you mean, Detective?" Cottrell played innocent." Who do you suspect?"

"We both know that Singleton killed his wife. You know it, I know it, and the priest knows it. As a matter of fact, the priest has heard his confession. Of that I'm certain."

Cottrell looked at Reese. "Did Father Wallace tell you this?"

"No. I was hoping you would."

"I don't know anything about that, Detective," he said. He ran his hand along the edge of the desk drawer where he had placed the letter the priest had given him. He didn't know why he had kept it, didn't put it in the coffin like Gene told him to do. Nor had he read it.

"I'm sure you do, Cottrell. Being you're so close to Gene Wallace. Buddies, I hear. Drinking buddies?"

Cottrell laughed a humorless chortle. "Well, the both of us tried AA at one time or the other but couldn't see much point in sticking to it. That's not a crime these days, is it, Detective? It's in my home, after all. We might consume a bit too much at times like most people," he said chuckling again, "but we're not committing a crime. And Gene is a priest, so he's not going to tell me anything that goes on in confession."

"But he might've let something slip—you know something, I could bet on that, and withholding evidence from the police is a crime."

"Maybe you don't understand honor and duty. Gene Wallace is my friend. His priesthood has significance for him that you and I wouldn't understand, Detective.

I would not ask him to reveal it if he indeed *had* heard a confession."

"I've come here to simply ask you for what we call justice, Cottrell. Someone should pay for the crime, and Bill Singleton is guilty of murder. I don't care what the Church says about the confessional."

"Maybe so. But maybe that man is already paying for his crime. Did you ever think of that?"

"He should go to jail, Cottrell, "Reese said with finality.

"There are all sorts of ways one pays for one's sins. Wouldn't you say so, Detective?"

Reese rose to go.

"If you change your mind, you know where to reach me."

"I'd like to help you, Detective Reese, but … it's not in my power."

Reese turned at the door of the office. "Don't bother to show me out."

John Cottrell sat there for a long time, his elbows on the desk, his head resting on his hands. Could he be arrested for obstructing justice? He let his head fall to the desk and let it linger there on the cool glass top while he wondered about the letter inside his desk. He was almost asleep when the phone woke him.

8

Wendell

The detective was a cold one, he thought. When they brought Wendell in for questioning, the young man had been so stunned that Patsy was dead, he dropped his usual defensive tactics and simply told the truth, his voice breaking with emotion.

"It was in the afternoon, after our session. I was trying to get her to let me drive her home, but she wouldn't."

"When did you leave the office?" Reese asked.

"Well, I hung around for bit after I left at 5:00 p.m.... She ... well, she was on the phone with somebody. I listened, tried to get a feel for who it was."

"Why would you do that?" Reese asked.

"It was just that it was somebody important to her. I was curious. I think it might have been somebody she was having an affair with. Don't ask me how I know—I just know. It was the tone of her voice. It wasn't her husband; that was for sure."

"Did you know about the gun?"

"What gun?"

"The .22 that killed her."

"No. I didn't have a gun— "

"You didn't know Ms. Singleton kept one in the office?"

"No, I didn't," he said, surprised. "But since she stayed there late at night sometimes, I guess it was understandable that she would."

"Your fingerprints are all over that office," Reese said.

"Well, I was her patient—court ordered. I was there every week for I don't know how long. Why wouldn't my fingerprints be there?"

"You left town right after. Why did you run?"

"I didn't run. I told her I was leaving. Keeping one step ahead of the law. You know how it is, Detective. I didn't kill her. As a matter of fact, I was with my girlfriend that night. She'll testify. You can't pin a murder wrap on me. And Patsy Singleton's murder at that. I really *liked* her, Detective. That woman was special. She was … cool actually. I even wanted to take her out—I offered her a ride home, but she sort of laughed at me, kind of flirty, didn't turn me down flat, but you know."

"And when she refused?"

"You got it all wrong. I didn't murder her," he almost screamed at the detective.

"Calm down, son. I'm just asking you some questions, that's all."

"I'm not a suspect?"

"I didn't say that. Until I get some more information from you, you might be."

"I had no reason to kill her," he said. He drummed his fingers on the table in the interrogation room. "She was something else, that woman," he said, his eyes misting. "I guess you could say I respected her even, and that's a lot coming from me, Detective—I don't have much use for therapists, psychologists and such. People who like to throw their education in your face, you know. People who think they know you, but they don't know a damn thing. But she—Ms. Singleton—she wasn't like that ... she was different from the others."

"Good looking—? "Reese offered.

"Well, yeah, for an older woman," he added." Sure, but— "

Reese smiled. "I hear tell you like older women." He got up to get himself a cup of coffee and offered Troy one, nodding at the cup.

The boy shook his head. "She was a real special lady. You know what I mean?"

"I'm beginning to see," Reese said, sipping the coffee. "So, did you hang around to see who showed up to meet her?"

"I wish I had, Detective," the boy said. "She might still be alive."

9

Les

"Rosemarie, I'm home!" Reese shouted when he entered the living room and shut the door behind him. He threw off his jacket, loosened his tie, and plopped into his easy chair. The house was silent. Where was she? Where were the boys? Oh, yes, he realized. Soccer practice. He was home much earlier than he had been the weeks since he'd been working on the Singleton murder. He sighed and turned on the TV, a Cincinnati station. It seemed like a different world, not like the hometown news of Mazewood where he worked, more like Chicago, but crime had made its way here, though not in such large doses. He thought again about his investigation. The chief was convinced Wendell Troy was guilty of the Singleton murder, even though his girlfriend insisted she'd spent the night with him. There was not enough evidence to bring it to trial. If they could only find the gun—for all he knew it was at the bottom of the Ohio River.

"Lester!" Rosemarie said, surprised to see him. The boys couldn't stop talking; first one and then the other had a story to tell about practice, their friends, their schoolwork. Soon he forgot about his own work and just enjoyed being at home. He helped Rosemarie in the kitchen. He beat the eggs for a frittata, an easy vegetarian meal they could have ready in less than an hour. He liked cooking, but he hadn't been home before dinner in weeks. Usually, he ate what was leftover from dinner—sometimes Rosie was even asleep by the time he got home.

"So, what's the deal on Ms. Singleton's murder, Les?"

"You don't want to hear about my work, do you? I want to forget about it for a while."

"You never forget, Les. I know you. You have it on your mind all the time, no matter what else you're doing—something with the kids, with me. Doesn't matter. You're always thinking about it. You can't let a cold case remain cold. Is it a cold case, Les?"

There was an edge to her voice he didn't much like, but it was true; he'd been neglecting her and the boys. "You know me that well, don't you?"

"Sure. It's OK. Talk about it to me if you can. I am sad that Ms. Singleton is dead, Les. She could have been my friend, and I miss her. She was so nice to me when nobody else was. She even bought my painting—you know the one—"

"I know. I saw it in her office."

"She hung it in her office?'

"Yeah," he said, looking at his wife's brown eyes, round and questioning.

"Did that boy do it?" she asked. "Did he kill her?"

"We never could pin anything about the murder on him, nor could we find the weapon—the gun Bill told us was there, the .22 he said he bought for her. It was gone."

"Did he *do* it, Les?" she said, turning to face him after she placed the dish into the oven. "Do *you* think he did it?"

"No. Troy didn't do it. He'll go to jail for possession of marijuana and trafficking drugs, and the chief is happy with that, just to get him off the streets."

"But you don't think he's the killer?"

Reese shook his head. "We would have broken him down if he were. I don't care how many alibis from his girlfriends he could come up with."

"Well, what about her boss, that Dr. Sweet? Maybe he's the one?"

Rosemarie checked on dinner in the oven and determined it was ready.

"No," he answered quietly.

"Hurry up, boys. It's time to eat," she called. "Wash your hands before you come to the table." Rosemarie was already distracted by the chattering of the boys, terminating their conversation about the killer for the moment, but Reese couldn't help turning it all around in his head again. Dr. Sweet, he thought, seemed like a nice enough guy, all broken up over Patsy's death; he seemed genuinely sorry for Bill through it all—and if he could be believed, had even reconciled with his wife since the murder. Reese didn't say anything else to Rosie about what his suspicions really were.

"Maybe if the case is cold," Rosemarie said suddenly to her silent husband later that evening, "then maybe you can get back to paying some attention to your family."

But Reese, in his determined way, continued to drop in on Bill Singleton now and then, keeping him abreast of Troy's trial, sometimes at the shop, sometimes at the house. It was his way. He could not let it go. He had seen the priest go in or come out of Bill's shop twice, and one day he nearly bumped into Father Wallace. He didn't think that was so unusual though. You were likely to see Gene Wallace just about anywhere—once he saw him at Ye Old Dutch Inn, a popular men's bar in town, buying a pint of vodka. And when someone made a remark about his frequent visits to the bar, Wallace just shrugged and laughed. "You're not likely to find the sinners at church," he said, grouping himself with the sinners in that odd, sad way of his.

For some months, and though it took quite a bit of his personal time, Detective Reese kept a close tab on Bill's activities. It was his theory, and simple police deduction, that the person closest to the victim was probably guilty. But Bill Singleton? Every other possibility had been thoroughly examined. The investigation uncovered that

Patsy Singleton had not been robbed—twenty dollars was still in her wallet—nor had she been raped, and there was no indication that a struggle of any kind had taken place.

Once Reese even followed Singleton all the way to Cleveland, which turned out to be a coin show. Reese had remained behind him on the highway, tailing him at a respectable distance in an unmarked police car. The prosecuting attorney had no interest in pursuing Bill by dragging out a cold case, and it had been filed as such, so Reese was on his own time. Nothing unusual occurred in Cleveland, except that Bill packed up and left early, not even setting up his wares. Reese went into the show, hoping to remain out of sight while he tailed Bill. He was even wearing jeans and a sweatshirt to try to blend in. Reese became interested in some of the coins and wound up losing his prey momentarily. Suddenly there was a familiar voice behind him. "What are you doing here, Detective?"

Reese turned and saw Bill in a rumpled suit, his satchel in his hand, an accusatory look on his face.

"Actually, I have an interest in Civil War things," he said, making it up to cover himself, but a little embarrassed that he, the policeman, had been discovered.

"So, why don't you come around to the shop sometime," he said. "I can show you a few special pieces. I don't believe I've ever seen you even looking before."

"Well, it's not a *real* hobby, just a curiosity, Bill."

Bill looked at him strangely, picked up his satchel from the floor and abruptly left the building. Reese followed at what he hoped was an unobtrusive distance and waited outside the hotel, watching Bill's window from his car, cold, drinking Dunkin Donuts coffee all night and cursing himself that he hadn't stayed home with Rosemarie.

Bill returned to Mazewood, apparently without making any contact with buyers or sellers. No hobnobbing at the hotel bar, no going out to dinner with anybody. It was odd behavior, even for Bill. He kept completely to himself, as he had done in town for months, hardly speaking to anyone.

Reese began frequenting the deli in town instead of going home to Rosie for lunch as usual. He knew Bill came in for a sandwich now and then, and while he waited, the detective listened for stories about him when he didn't show. Sometimes people would make jokes about Bill, his oddness, his ineptness in sociability—sometimes it would go on for quite a while and then suddenly stop when Bill ambled in—he never seemed to notice how suddenly quiet it had become, as he sat alone in a corner, ate his sparse lunch, answered a question if someone asked, but otherwise said little. The patrons of the deli would go on talking about the latest juicy gossip, finally ignoring Bill altogether. Soon the coin dealer ceased to make any trips out of town at all or show up at the deli. The weather had become cold, and snow threatened. A new baseball card sign came down from the dusty window and another with large red letters in an amateur hand read, "Antiques."

One day when Reese stopped in the shop to chat, he found that Bill looked considerably thinner. His clothes, always baggy and misshapen, literally hung on him. "Been on a diet, Bill?" he asked casually, looking at the coin dealer's face, which was now lined and paler than when he'd last seen him. Reese removed an empty cardboard box from a hardback chair, the only one in the shop, and sat down leaning back against the wall. He looked all around him at the furniture stuffed into the tiny office.

"Have a seat, Lester," Bill Singleton said to him, after the fact and, if the truth be known, Reese thought, rather sarcastically.

Reese opened his overcoat and reached inside his jacket pocket for his pipe. Though he had given up smoking cigarettes, he still could not bring himself to shed the tobacco habit completely. Rosie didn't let him light up inside the house, so he saved the pleasure for times like this. One of his boys, the younger one, had asthma. "Mind if I smoke?" he asked, match in hand.

Singleton shook his head no but looked agitated, as if he could not wait for the visitor to leave.

"Am I keeping you from something, Bill?" he asked politely but with no intention of curtailing his visit.

Singleton sighed but shook his head no. "I'm expecting a client soon," he said, distractedly. Again, he brought the silver dollar out of his pocket and turned it nervously round and round in his hand, looking out the window and then down at the coin in his hand as if he'd find something new there.

Reese watched him for a moment and then his eyes wandered over to the grandfather clock made of fine wood that stood near the corner in front of the brick wall; he had seen it in Singleton's house in the hallway entrance. And that hall tree piece too. Other items were piled on a cherry drop leaf table the detective recognized as well. He had a good memory for details. There was hardly room to turn around in the confined space. "Why are you selling all these antiques, Bill?" he asked casually, before he lit a match and began sucking in on the pipe stem. The already stuffy room began to fill with the sweet aroma of Captain Black tobacco, a mild but pleasant blend.

Singleton closed his eyes and sighed, letting his impatience with the detective show. "I'm just getting rid of them, Lester, if that's all right with you?" His sarcasm took Reese aback for a moment. "They're my property, aren't they? I can do what I want with them."

"Just asking," Reese said, holding up his hand as a peace signal. "You can sell any damn thing you want."

"There's too much in the house that reminds me of Patsy, that's all," Bill explained, almost apologetically now. "I ... I just want to ... redecorate. That's it. I just want to *redecorate*," he said, savoring the word as if it meant something special to him. "Get rid of all the *old* stuff and buy new. That's it ... buy new." A faint smile passed his lips almost as an afterthought.

"Well," Reese said, "you ought to get a pretty good price on some of these items." He ran his hand appreciatively over the edge of the drop leaf table. Dust covered his fingers. Reese thought it strange how he vacillated between an odd pity for Singleton, the man, and an abhorrence for someone who could murder his wife. "Rosie—my wife—might be interested in this piece, Bill. What's the price?"

Bill looked at him blankly. After a long pause he finally said, "Best offer."

"Actually, Rosie's into more modern stuff. You know, like her paintings." Reese gave a little laugh, and said, "Occasionally she buys an interesting old table or some odd little thing and makes it work together. Women are something, aren't they?"

Singleton nodded. "Yeah. Women never do know what they want. Hard to tell what they want. They change ... you know?" He searched Lester's face for an element of empathy, the detective supposed.

Reese coughed, clearing his throat and nodding. "I know what you mean."

"About the table, I—I'm just looking for the best offer," Bill Singleton said in his most business-like voice. "I'm sure I'll never get anywhere near what Patsy paid for it."

"I'll send Rosemarie around," Reese said when he rose to go. Then he turned back to face the pale and lined visage of the rapidly aging coin dealer, his hand still on the door handle. It was hard to believe he and this man were the same age. "You're getting too thin, Bill. Don't be skipping so many lunches. I never see you at the deli anymore."

"I guess I forget to eat sometimes," was the only thing the lean, melancholy man could say.

Reese nodded and turned to go. "By the way, Bill, I got a call from Sheriff Baxter in Abington. Wants to know why your car's been parked over there so often, near that brick ranch house you used to own."

Bill seemed surprised and at a loss for an answer.

Lester closed the door he had partially opened. "The folks that are living there now have been complaining like a son of gun."

"Complaining?"

"Well, yeah. Somebody parked near a house that has young children playing outside all the time. What do you think? Wouldn't you be suspicious?"

"I guess I didn't think about that. I didn't mean anyone any harm, Lester."

"They complain you just sit there and look at the house. You shouldn't spend so much time over there," Lester advised. "It looks ... weird.... you know." Then he opened the door again to the blustering cold, exited the building, and pulled the door shut behind him. Once he was outside, he buttoned up his overcoat against the wind and the light snow that was beginning to fall. Lester Reese headed back to the police station.

In April, another call came in from Abington, but Reese had been knee-deep into another case and didn't learn about it until he came on duty in the morning. In the middle of the night, Singleton had tried to bury his dog Bundy in the backyard of the Abington house— that old dog had finally died—Someone in the residence awoke around 3:00 a.m. and saw a light in the backyard. It turned out to be Bill's snake light wrapped around a fence. The deputy sheriff arrived to find the dog wrapped in a blanket and Bill still digging a hole with a shovel. They took Bill in and held him overnight, but Sheriff Baxter, surmising that he needed some other kind of help, asked Bill what church he belonged to. That was when they called the priest from St. Ann's. Lester Reese arrived after he did.

10

Les

It was Father Wallace who talked the sheriff out of pressing charges before Lester arrived.

"Isn't this beyond your territory, Father?" Reese asked the bedraggled priest. His eyes were bloodshot, and he looked as if he hadn't been to bed at all.

"Oh, I was awake all night … still at a parishioner's home. They got me on my cell phone," the assistant pastor explained. "There was no need for them to wake you and bring you all the way down here, Detective Reese. It isn't even your jurisdiction."

Reese looked at the priest, and when their eyes met, he saw defiance there.

"The charges have been dropped—everything is fine," Father Wallace said.

"Just checking to make sure Bill is all right," Reese said.

"He's just having a hard time, Detective. Wouldn't you? His wife's death has taken a serious toll on him."

The thickness of his speech told Reese the priest had been drinking. "Do you think you should be driving, Father?"

"I'll take him home now," The priest said icily. He took Singleton's arm and led him down the hall, heading toward the parking lot. And Bill gave no resistance.

"Wait a minute. Wait just a minute!" Reese shouted.

"Bill," he said, grabbing his arm and turning him around. "What have *you* got to say about all this?"

Reese couldn't help but notice that the emaciated coin dealer had lost more weight, if that were possible, and could not seem to focus attention on what Reese was saying. It was a wonder the man could be living, he was so thin.

"What the hell happened here?"

"Didn't the sheriff tell you?" the priest intoned. "If he thought it so necessary to call you, he must have told you what happened."

The vitriol in the remark took Lester aback for a moment. "Let him answer the question," Reese demanded, vying for some control he felt he was losing.

But Bill Singleton was so foggy he was non-communicative; he would answer no questions, *could* answer none at this point, he supposed.

"The man simply needs to go home," Father Wallace said impatiently. "You're not helping matters by standing here in the hallway when he's already been released."

"You go on home, Father. I'll take care of getting

Singleton home." He used a tone that never failed to shake up the young officers on the force. But he thought the priest relented, not because he was afraid of Reese, but because he too, was so exhausted. Where had he been? At whose house at this time of night? Then he remembered that the Catholics had that last rights sacrament. What was it called? Extreme Unction. He was probably performing one of those kinds of sacraments. Drunk as he was, he was trying to fulfill some duty.

"Father, I'm really sorry," he said. "I've been on edge lately. You must be tired. Why don't you let me take both you and Singleton home? I can have your car delivered to the rectory tomorrow."

The priest did not stop or acknowledge Reese's change in attitude until they all reached his car in the parking lot.

"No, no," he said. "The Pink Lady and I are just fine." His hand shook as he unlocked the door of the aging pink station wagon, a gift from the parish that he affectionately named after the Blessed Mother. He still gently held onto Bill's bony arm.

Father Wallace gave Reese a long serious look. "It's quite all right, Detective," he said. "I know you mean to do your job, but—"

"All right, then it's settled. You're coming with me, Bill," Reese said. Both the detective and the priest knew Wallace could be arrested on the spot on a DUI charge. Reese was pretty sure he could get a positive reading on a test, even though he couldn't detect the vodka by smelling his breath. "I'll follow you past the rectory, Father," Reese stated flatly.

The priest answered him with silence. To Bill he said, "William, I'll see you in church. And good luck to you, sir," he addressed Reese with a half salute. Still pondering the priest's peculiar remark, Reese watched him get inside the station wagon and, without the least hesitation, speed out of the parking lot.

Bill Singleton got inside Reese's Buick, while the detective held the door open. What had he meant by "Good luck," Les wondered? That priest was obstinate, a trial, a real "hard nut to crack," but he would have to call him principled in some weird way—at least in the eyes of his church. He had tried to get it out of Rosie what it meant, this "seal of the confessional." She thought it was perfectly easy to understand and couldn't see how Lester didn't get it. "The Church is a sanctuary," she explained. "A haven."

"I know that but—"

"No, you don't see," she objected, vehemently. Rosemarie could get all fired up over a religion she had left years ago if somebody said something that was incorrect, or someone was under a wrong impression about it. "One should have the security of being able to tell a priest *anything* in confession and he won't ... no he *can't* blab it to anybody. Not if he is a real priest." Rosie's dark eyes had shone as she defended the priest's position. She was so passionate about everything, and so good for an aging, jaded policeman. He loved her even more for the things he could not quite grasp about her.

"I'm not asking him to blab to anyone else, Rosie—People in society have an obligation to help the police."

"It doesn't matter, Les," she said in her soft Columbian accent. "The priest, he answers to a higher authority than you guys can ever be." She always teased him with her answers, acting as if he was the foreigner, and in this realm he really was. What did he know about the Church and its mysteries? Its people were mysteries, including Rosie.

At the house, when Reese had interrogated Bill before, he had once heard him refer to it ironically as "Patsy's Pride." Looking at it from Bill's viewpoint, the house was a monster that continually had to have something done to it to keep it up to par, let alone to make it into the showplace Patsy Singleton wanted it to be.

Mrs. Singleton, were she alive on that day Lester took the would-be criminal home from Abington, would have been appalled, to say the least, at the condition of her house. Dog smell and dog urine nearly knocked him over as soon as he entered the door. The next thing he noticed, even with his coat on, was that it was so cold inside. Lights didn't work either. Of course, he hadn't—perhaps had even forgotten—to pay the bills. Bill stood looking around him as if he did not know where he was.

"Bill," Reese shouted, trying to get the man's attention. "Listen, Bill! Have you got a flashlight in the kitchen? Or … candles? Anything to see by?"

Singleton turned slowly to look at the detective, but Reese knew he was not comprehending the words.

"I'm going outside to the car for a flashlight. Sit down on the couch—if there is one. Anyway, relax," he demanded. "I'll be back."

Bill nodded and stood where he was.

When Reese returned, a flashlight burning in his hand, Bill began to talk: "I had to bury Bundy in our back yard, near the house. Bundy was such a good dog. He and Allen were the best of friends. Allen will be so sad that he's dead."

"But that was the second dog," Reese reminded him. "You called him Bundy, too?"

When the first one died, Bill had bought a replacement and given the dog the same name as the first one. Reese had gotten the story from the priest, who had remembered because Allen was an altar boy at the church when the first one died. Father Wallace had tried to comfort the twelve-year-old boy, but it was Allen's first experience with death, and he seemed inconsolable until the second dog, exactly like the first, was purchased and named.

Bill suddenly babbled something about seeing if Patsy was home and Reese watched him slowly mount the stairs. A moment later he followed him into the bedroom where Bill curled up on the bed with no sheets, only a mattress. It was probably the last stick of furniture left in the house that Bill had not sold yet or burned for firewood, apart from the gun cabinet standing upright in the corner. That no doubt would be gone soon. Reese searched a closet and found a blanket. Covering the wasted figure, he stood there watching him until he heard the slow, steady breathing of sleep, and then he walked down the long stairway with the flashlight beam in front of him. He examined the living room, running the flashlight over the ashes piled up under the grate of the fireplace. Not much remained, only the curtains and some piled-up newspapers. Then he went into the kitchen.

The squalor was appalling. Dog food cans sat open on the counter and unwashed dishes might have been in the sink for six months, they were so caked with old food. Reese gagged when he opened the refrigerator. He found plastic bags and, without hesitating, began throwing things in them. When he had gathered up all the debris and carried the bags outside, he put them in garbage cans and dragged them to the curb for pickup in the morning.

Back in the kitchen he washed the dishes in the sink, the flashlight shining from the window ledge. In the morning he would call social services. He halted his hands in the sudsy water for a moment and stared at a dead plant beside the flashlight. It had once been a lively flower, but it had withered and was now brown and so hard when he touched it, it broke and crumbled to dust.

11

Cottrell

Cottrell came up behind Detective Reese and put his hand on his shoulder, but his eyes remained on the corpse in the casket, admiring his handiwork. "Shocking thing, isn't it, Lester?" He shook his head back and forth and clicked his tongue. "Terrible thing."

His hand was still on the detective's shoulder when Reese spotted Allen and his young family standing and greeting those who arrived to show their respects.

"Allen—he must have been shocked—" Reese began.

"Father Wallace had called Allen but—"

"Wallace, huh?"

"Well, he's their priest, isn't he?"

"He's more than their priest, I'd say," Reese answered.

Cottrell looked at him sideways. "His son had not known, nor even suspected what was going on. Father Wallace was trying to make it easier for him."

"Wallace meddles, if you ask me," Reese said.

Cottrell sighed. "Too bad there was no family near to

look out for him in his time of trouble, isn't it, Lester?" He was speaking softly, smoothly, in that cultivated voice of his. "The boy, of course, didn't know, hadn't realized the full extent of his father's illness—otherwise he would have come home sooner." Cottrell's stomach protruded out over his belt, but he kept his dark green jacket smoothed down over it. "Yes, it's a real shame— first Patsy Ann, and now Bill. Both needless, unnecessary deaths, don't you think so?

The detective stared at him but didn't answer.

"What do you make of it, Lester—as a detective, I mean?"

Cottrell could see Lester's irritation. How he wished him away. How he was just a hair away from solving this murder and then Bill went and died on him.

"I could deduce who the murderer was; I just couldn't prove it," Reese said.

"Not deducible by normal means," Cottrell said. "Only a hunch?"

"I always had a feeling you knew something more than you were telling, Cottrell, you and your buddy, Gene. What do you bury in the bottom of those bottles of vodka?"

Mourners came to the casket and Cottrell quietly led Reese aside and the two of them moved away from the body.

"Too many questions you couldn't find an answer to?" Cottrell said. "Why was the gun never recovered?"

Lester merely shook his head. They were both silent for a few minutes.

"Heart failure, that's what the doctor's report said," Cottrell volunteered, nodding at the corpse. "Malnutrition and about a million other things nobody knew about," he added.

Reese nodded. "How'd you do it?" he asked.

"What?"

"Make him look like he hadn't starved himself to death, hadn't died of cold and loneliness, or lack of love—or whatever else happened to the poor miserable son of a bitch. He almost has a smile on his face, for Chrissakes, Cottrell," Reese said through his teeth.

"Why that's a trade secret, detective," Cottrell said, an amused smile playing about his lips. Guess you have yours too." Then he chuckled softly, perhaps inappropriately but so as not to be heard by the mourners. "Damned *sad* situation, real *sad*," he repeated without humor.

12

Les

Reese stayed and knelt with the few people who remained for the rosary. It felt odd but he forced himself to do it. He listened to Father Wallace's voice, masculine in depth but softly effeminate too, rising and falling over the Our Fathers and Hail Marys, ritual-like and monotonous. He wondered if Gene Wallace believed Bill would go to hell because he had not confessed to authorities and made restitution for his sins, or perhaps he had confessed again at the last minute and that absolved him. Why hadn't he helped him do that by turning him in? Singleton would at least be alive today if he had. Catholics were an odd lot, he thought. Even Rosie.

Cottrell took Reese by the arm after Allen and the others said their last goodbyes to the deceased. "Come," he said. "I'm about to close the viewing room."

"Where's Father Wallace?" Reese asked, looking around the room. He hadn't seen him go out the door.

"He's back in my office … I told Allen not to go back

to the house," he said, "—to stay in the motel—It's too depressing in that damned old house and it smells. It'll give him the creeps. Going in to get the body was an experience, let me tell you! Not even a bed left in there to sleep on."

Reese swallowed and braced himself against something, he did not know what. "Where'd you find him?" he asked.

"On the floor near the fireplace. Poor soul. Soot all over the place. They said he sold off *everything*, all that fine furniture. Just managing to pay some of the bills—and the rent on the shop."

Reese wondered if he had sold the gun too. He had stopped in periodically at the shop. He had examined the tiny place thoroughly early on, after he and the officer had been to the house. And Reese had a pretty good eye for summing up what was in the place on his visits. There was no safety deposit box at the bank or anything like that.

"God forbid he shouldn't pay rent on that dusty old place he called a business," Cottrell remarked, shaking his head and clicking his tongue again. "Can you imagine? Sold off every stick of Patsy's antiques too—what he didn't burn for firewood to keep warm. God knows it wasn't for food. When they found him—social services—somebody called them. By the time they got around to it, he'd been dead a couple of days already."

"Why do you suppose he let this happen?" Reese

asked, a rhetorical question really—he didn't expect an answer.

Cottrell shrugged. He locked the front door and turned off the lights in the viewing room. "Come on back into my office, Lester. Gene and I are just going to have a little libation to ward off the winter chill. Won't you join us?"

Lester's first impulse was to say no, that he had to get home to Rosemarie, that his wife was all excited about getting the floor plans for the old house they bought, and she wanted to show him some "secrets" the walls held, whatever that meant. Something made him hesitate and accept the undertaker's invitation, putting his "work" as it were, ahead of his home life. "Why thanks, John. Don't mind if I do," Reese said, his hat still in his hand. "I'm officially off-duty this evening, so I guess it's all right."

Cottrell got out shot glasses from the bottom drawer. "Absolut okay?" he asked.

Reese nodded.

The undertaker poured. "Some people want to put things inside the casket when someone dies, things they think the dead person might want to take on with them into the next life."

"Did Bill take anything with him, John?" Father Wallace asked quietly.

"Well, I've put everything from cigars, jewelry, letters; you name it, inside with the dead bodies if somebody asked me to. But nobody said what was to go to the grave with Bill. I found an old two-headed silver coin in his pocket … and I let him keep it."

The other two held their glasses, waiting.

13

Cottrell

There was a letter too, Cottrell recalled, but didn't say it aloud—The letter stayed sealed, in his desk, meant for Patsy in a handwriting he was familiar with—but he hadn't read it, nor did he put it inside her coffin as he was instructed to do—That, too, would remain a secret. Now, Bill would take that letter with him, along with the coin. He deserved the truth.

14

Les

Reese was watching when the priest swallowed and closed his eyes as if in prayer. The small office was warm and suddenly it felt very much like the white walls with the pictures of the Sacred Heart and Michael the Archangel and the crucifix above Cottrell's head were about to close in on him, and still, he stayed.

"Here's to Bill, the coin dealer," Cottrell said, raising his shot glass. The priest and detective raised their glasses with him. "To Bill Singleton," Reese said.

"May his soul and the soul of Patsy Ann rest in peace," Father Wallace prayed before he downed the fiery liquid.

Reese sipped his in silence. Finally, he said, "He *did* it, of course."

The two men were silent, waiting for him to continue.

"I can't figure where the gun went. That's the only thing I just can't figure. What did he do with it? It's not in the mighty Ohio. Bill wouldn't have thrown the gun away. Somehow I know he still had it somewhere." The other two were mute.

"He *did* it, I know he did," Lester said. "Killed Patsy Ann as sure as I'm sitting here, but it wouldn't have done any good to arrest him. No good at all. Couldn't bring it to court. Not enough evidence to make it stick." He shook his head and sighed.

"I followed him," Lester continued. "I pursued him, dammit! I tried to trip him up, to get him to confess. But he just got thinner and more silent."

Cottrell poured another round for himself and Gene. Lester was still sipping.

"I just couldn't figure what he did with the damned *gun*." A silence fell on the three, and two of them flung back their heads to receive the second shot.

Finally, the priest said, "It's a divine mystery to us all." Then he added, "Only the walls know for sure, Detective Reese. Only the walls, as the saying goes."

Cottrell ignored Wallace's oblique remark. "No, I guess it wouldn't have done any good to send poor old Bill to jail, even if you could have gotten a conviction. Looks like he's finally punished himself enough for it anyway—if he really did do it. What would you say, Father Wallace? Is Bill guilty?" A twinkle gleamed in Cottrell's eye when he goaded the priest.

Gene Wallace stared at the last drop of the clear liquid that remained in his glass. "We're all guilty, gentlemen," he said with a sad smile. "We're all guilty as hell."

• *CAROL MAURIELLO*

ACKNOWLEDGMENTS

Thank you, Katerina Stoykova, for selecting my story to be published by Accents. I am grateful for your decision to have a novella contest, which was the vehicle responsible for getting me there.

Also, I would like to thank the Foothills Writers, who have been my writer's group and my support for many years.

• *CAROL MAURIELLO*

ABOUT THE AUTHOR

Carol Mauriello lives near The Daniel Boone National Forest in Olive Hill, Kentucky with her husband, Joe. She is a native of Kentucky who returned to her home state after living in New York and New Jersey for 25 years. She is retired from teaching English at Morehead State University. Her stories, poems, essays, and novels expand over a wide variety of experiences and locales. She has written one unpublished novel and is currently at work on a novel about a young man in recovery from a schizoaffective illness, and who has chosen to live in a New Jersey Beach town.

* 9 7 8 1 9 3 6 6 2 8 8 5 8 *